Expiration Date: a Short Story Collection

Bert Whirl

Published by Red Tree Publishing, 2023.

This is a work of fiction. Similarities to real people, places, or events are entirely coincidental.

EXPIRATION DATE: A SHORT STORY COLLECTION

First edition. July 1, 2023.

Copyright © 2023 Bert Whirl.

ISBN: 979-8223646846

Written by Bert Whirl.

Table of Contents

Special thanks to JH, MD, KJ, CB, JG, AM, and all those others who helped me get this collection together.

Visiting Rebecca

Juan stood on the dirt path near the curb, holding a single yellow rose. His thoughts rehearsed what he would say as he gazed along the path and past the iron fence.

His fingers rolled the flower in his hand, which drew his gaze down to follow the petals. He sniffed and drew his sleeve across his nose. He'd brought a bouquet of these to Rebecca's house their last night together. Their three-month anniversary.

For those three months, she had insisted they meet anywhere but her house, but felt after this long, this visit might prove safe. Her dad had tried to chase him off. Rebecca snuck out to see Juan, anyway. They had gone to an empty parking lot to talk, not expecting that to be their last night together. They'd spoken of hopes and plans over the weeks they'd been seeing each other. Even on that night.

A stupid drunk driver jumped the curb and changed everything.

Rebecca danced into his mind's eye. Her round face with the room-brightening smile always melted his heart. He'd forget what he wanted to say when she gazed at him. Her being held so much beyond her face, though. She loved to twirl and dance, especially in her sun dresses. She'd worn a light yellow dress with darker yellow roses for their last date. And she'd sworn the color and flower were her favorites.

Her family had created a small memorial dedicated to her in their side yard. Juan had helped plant a yellow rosebush in her memory. But Rebecca's father had refused to help while Juan had remained.

In his head, her image twirled back. She stood on her front porch, wearing that same yellow sundress with the roses stenciled throughout the fabric. It was modest by sundress standards, reaching to mid shin and covering her arms to mid biceps. It hung on her with a perfect silhouette, not too tight but not too loose.

Juan drew a deep breath and released it as a long sigh through his nose.

On mild days, she'd wear this faint rosy perfume. He always loved her scent–that rare rose aroma she had found in a small boutique downtown. It took Juan a week to find where she'd bought it so he could give her the gift.

He'd brought a box with him on his last visit. However, Rebecca's family had arrived before him, and her dad wouldn't let him approach, wouldn't let him leave anything for her. Juan had to smuggle his gift to her through Rebecca's sister. Juan swore after that to always make his visits when he knew her family wouldn't also be visiting.

Thoughts of Rebecca pulled his feet along the path.

After four steps, Juan stopped. He stared at the iron gate. His hand reached for the barrier, but it hovered over the cold metal. No matter how much he practiced, he didn't feel ready. No matter how often he visited, it always hurt to see her. These struggles never appeared when he visited his grandparents. Pivoted on his heels, he walked back to the street. As he reached the curb, Juan stopped, wiped away his tears, and drew a deep breath. People expected him to visit her, no matter if his own emotions were ready.

Juan fought his own reluctance, turned himself around, and hauled himself back to the iron gate. His gaze followed the path beyond the gate. They'd added solar path lights since his last visit to his grandparents. Others sat on benches near loved ones, talking and crying. He understood. If he got past this visit, he knew he could continue to come see her.

Pushing on the gate, Juan stepped through the fence opening and followed the path. The path traveled through a quiet gathering of memorials and floral arrangements. He neared his desired section and saw he didn't visit alone. He walked around a corner and saw Rebecca's little sister, Jennifer, standing beside the path and holding a dozen yellow roses. Her body shook as she soaked the flowers with her tears. While Juan wanted to stay back from her, he also knew she needed a shoulder as much as he did.

Jennifer pulled her gazed over to Juan when he approached. She had a younger version of Rebecca's face, but with puffy and bloodshot eyes. They'd been close. He walked to her side, and she leaned against him. Placing his arm around her shoulders, Juan offered what comfort he could, though he didn't find the same comfort within himself.

They stood there, each crying but lost in their own thoughts for five minutes. Jennifer pulled back and wiped a gloved hand across her cheeks, smearing the already running make-up. She attempted a weak smile, and Juan returned the effort. Grief, even after months, killed smiles as one worked through it. Juan realized that all he'd rehearsed made no difference. He didn't need to say anything.

Juan held out his arm, hoping that Jennifer might take his elbow. Jennifer slid her hand onto the provided arm. They stepped off the path and onto the fresh-laid sod. As they stood there, Juan released Jennifer's hand so he could step forward.

He leaned down and brushed his lips across the top of Rebecca's granite gravestone. His rose rolled in his fingers before he placed it on the raised dirt of her grave. The faded box of perfume leaned against the grave marker, cradled by a teddy bear with equal amounts of fading. Juan lingered and let his fingers trace Rebecca's name. A light breeze pushed against Juan, like Rebecca reminding him to share. Small droplets of rain fell as Jennifer echoed Juan's movements. Her tears mixed with the rain above Rebecca's head. With their deliveries complete, they shuffled around to stand at Rebecca's feet and gaze at her plot. Tears ran down Juan's cheeks and he left them there. The tears presented his best apology. Juan and Jennifer leaned against each other, holding back the grief with their company.

Five minutes in the rain felt like an eternity. To stand and talk to those one lost. They slid apart to walk the path back to the cemetery's fence border. At the gate, Juan and Jennifer shared one last hug before going to their own cars.

Investment of Spirits

I stretched my bolt cutters toward the door's padlock. My entire being shook as I held back my glee. My partner and I snagged this well-placed apartment building a month ago. We could convert it into a veritable goldmine. The building had remained on the market, vacant, for a decade. After that long, I expected the building's interior required work. Grand plans bubbled through my head. Those plans hijacked my thoughts. However, before I could go on, someone interrupted my joy.

"Don't cut it," my partner said. "We shouldn't go in there."

I'd forgotten he traveled to the building with me. I frowned as I turned, moving the bolt cutters down and away from the lock. My eyes narrowed and my voice gained a frustrated edge. "Why the heck not? It's a perfectly suitable building that needs to be readied for tenants."

"You're blind, I swear." My partner shook his head and pointed past my head to the door window. "The Spirit Patrol sealed this building. That sticker means either a hostile ghost, a bad power flow, or some untoward supernatural thing exists within the building. And they couldn't fix it." He stepped back. "That makes things bad."

"Spirit Patrol?" I said. Dragging my eyes from my partner, I examined the gold ghost sticker with a large red X across it. Derision filled my voice as I stepped away from the door. "The frauds bilking people of their money and claiming to have done something miraculous within the supernatural realm? Real life 'Ghostbusters'?"

While shaking my head, I returned to my task as I muttered about the bane of superstitious people upon society. My hands positioned the bolt cutters against the lock. I'd lost my extreme joy and became frustrated. That had eased my shakes. But not my anxiousness to enter the building. Opening the handles, I tensed my muscles. A quick shove would clamp the blades closed.

"If you cut that lock, our deal is off," my partner said. He seemed quieter. The cutters lowered again so I could find him. He stood in the parking lot, in a handicapped space, fifty feet away.

"Are you serious? You can't back out now," I said, my voice rising so my partner could hear me. "We have a written contract, signed and notarized. Half the investment is in place."

"My lawyer can find an out clause. I'm not crossing that building's threshold," my partner said. He opened his car door and climbed into the driver's seat. To defy expectations, he didn't start the car. I shrugged. More money for me.

Enough stalling, I told myself. Spinning on my heels, I faced my prize. My cutters rose into place with no hesitation. I chopped the lock and watched it fall to the ground with a soft thud. Not sure why I didn't grab it with my hand, but I used my cutters to pry the remaining lock flange off the door's bar. It wobbled as the door came free from its confinement. After I leaned the cutters against the wall, I reached for the door handle.

When my hand wrapped around the door handle, the building creaked. The foundation couldn't still be settling. This building had occupied this spot for over one hundred and fifty years. Even as I examined the building's walls, I couldn't think of any other valid explanation. Again, I shrugged.

I applied pressure to the door handle, intent on pulling it open. The door swung into the building's foyer. It allowed me my first glimpse into my future goldmine.

That first view didn't overwhelm me. They'd lined the small entryway with mailboxes along the left wall. A small reception desk and a sweeping staircase filled the open space beyond. Original blueprints suggested the building had an open courtyard. The previous owners had enclosed it for security reasons. Our plans for the space hadn't reached the discussion of reopening it. That decision rested on the cost for heating and cooling the two-story room.

Previous owners had added a refined touch to the room's floor. They'd laid porcelain tiles, though I saw chipped and cracked spots from use and the weather. I'd need to have a contractor repair those.

Leaning in, I checked the lobby's centerpiece. My whistle echoed off the walls of the large room as I gazed at the ceiling. The crystal chandelier occupied most of the entryway's second story space. Power and cleaning would make it sparkle. The sun would create rainbows as the crystal glittering. That grand image gave me a new type of shake.

Somewhere on the first floor, I'd need an office, or I'd need to convert one apartment to an office, but that wasn't a big deal. I raised my foot to step through the threshold and stand within my new building.

Something bounced off the back of my left knee and clattered along the ground. The strike drew my attention, so I pulled myself around from the entrance. I gazed down at the small plastic ice scraper that lay on the sidewalk. Naturally, my gaze rose toward my partner, who now sat on his car's hood. His frantic gestures tried to pull me away from the building.

"I'm still going in," I said. "Your tactics will only delay the inevitable." Picking up the ice scraper, I tossed it to my partner, then turned to face the portal to my financial freedom.

Right then, I hadn't detected a whiff of anything wrong. It's a pull door. But it swung into the room. My mind had wrapped itself in visions of the potential dollars I'd make, the things I'd do, and ignored everything else.

With a full body shake, I released any negative thoughts that clung to me and stepped into the building. My foot crushed a small piece of broken tile. Concerned for my shoes, I glanced down, but saw only a small piece of broken porcelain. It's easily replaceable. Or so I told myself, anyway. When I returned my gaze to the room, something shimmering stood on the second-floor stairs, walking from the balcony. That balcony might hold a good place to construct the building's gym. The shimmering I brushed away, thinking it a light trick through the dusty windows and chandelier. I took a second step forward, crushing another piece of tile.

The door slammed shut behind me. The dead bolt slid into place when it hit the doorframe. My head swivelled to examine the door, to see the attached spring. No spring existed. I saw no dead bolt, either, but I know I heard one slide and lock.

Only one direction remained available to me. I faced the room. And nearly jumped to the chandelier when I saw the shimmering forms floating in front of me. It felt as if my eyes played tricks on me.

A man's form hid within the yellowish light, its arms crossed over its chest. He looked nothing like my partner, like anyone I knew. I'd had the building checked for squatters and the local sheriff assured me no one lived here. I checked around me. No one entered with me. Since only I stood in this building, I felt no fear. But I felt unnerved.

The shimmering man advanced a step, so I mirrored him with a step back. Fortune remained, for the moment, as I didn't step on another tile piece. However, the figure of the man remained as close as a companion.

Time to do the proper, cowardly thing. Twisting around, I ran.

I slammed my weight against the door. It didn't budge. Of course, after two steps, I probably had no force behind me. The lighted man leaned against the wall. He laughed, though I couldn't hear him. It took a minute for my mind to register that I hadn't fallen. Trapped.

I spun against the door, used it to push off for momentum. I ran along the wall, dodged the reception desk, and stopped at the base of the stairs. Man shimmer paced me the entire way. When I arrived, he leaned against the newel post. Pivoting, I angled to dash up the stairs. Instead, I met two more shimmering people, arms crossed like the first one. They appeared bulkier and blocked my advance. Not going that way.

Escape proved elusive. Did the shimmering people exist as solid or diffuse? Don't care. They looked like holograms. I had difficulty telling the gender of the two blocking my path, unless I got close and personal. Didn't care enough to do that. Backing away from them, I bumped into a wall. To get away, I twisted toward the door, but I encountered shiny people blocking my every direction.

None of them looked entirely pleased to see me standing in the building, except the one who continued to lean against the newel post. They gave me space, allowed me a one foot by one foot square, but nothing more. Shifting my body, I tried to back away until I flattened against the wall. None of the shimmering assemblage moved for several moments. I guess they wanted to let the situation really settle into my consciousness. For all my denial of their ability and skills, I prayed for the spirit patrol, the ghost busters, anyone who could save my sorry butt.

I closed my eyes and slid down the wall. Something stopped me before I reached the floor. This wasn't the bottom stair, and I'd seen no bench against this wall. Whatever it was, it felt solid under me. I opened my left eye, looked down. Glowing like the people, a bench had formed beneath me as I sank. Seated beside me, I saw another of the shimmering men. Of note, my companion was not one of the group who'd confronted me. Moving its arm, the man put a hand on my knee and I discovered I could understand what he said.

"Why are you here, son?" Everything froze.

I didn't answer. My eyes locked on the hand that had settled on my knee. The fact it rested there sank past my shock, and I realized it felt as solid as the bench. About that point, my brain pushed to the front of my consciousness only logical thoughts. If this shimmering man touched me, and felt solid, he must exist. A simple man dressed in a glowing suit.

This theory held true until the man's hand slid to mid-thigh and sank into my leg. When the shimmering man repeated his question, it sounded louder and more commanding this time. "Why are you here, son?"

I found my voice at that point. "I bought the building and came to find its needed repairs and renovations. Make it ready for new tenants. My original plan was to bulldoze the place, rebuild it as a shiny new jewel, but the historic register kept me from that plan. So, I created an alternate plan, which called for gutting and renovation." My thoughts, my plans, flowed from my mouth like water, unable to stop once I began.

What made everything seem weirder, I felt more than I heard the other shimmering images' murmurs. Those feelings sent the sensation of thousands of allergy shots along my arms. The scent of sulfur reached my nose, but I didn't see any flames. Of course, my eyes didn't move from the spot where the hand sank inside my leg.

"This place could be huge, make aircraft-carrier-sized boats worth of cash. It just needs some work. Bring it up to code." Not daring to move, I stopped talking and waited. Murmurs flowed through my head, as if someone poured honey over the cereal of my mind.

"At least he's being honest," flowed a murmur I clearly understood. Taking major effort and willpower, I raised my eyes to consider the man's face next to me. His face looked drawn and gaunt, with a short beard around his chin and jawline. Tracing my eyes down, I noted his body appeared as drawn and gaunt as his face. My examination didn't affect my liaison with this group of people as he stared at me, waiting. Raising his free hand, he silenced the group. He leaned closer, so that his nose almost touched my cheek.

"Did you consider the residents who already owned homes within this building?" A statement as bold as that snapped my shock. I glared at the figure.

"No living residents still hold title to any space in this building," I said. "The previous deed holder passed away ten years ago with no heir to maintain the property. According to the state, I bought an abandoned building."

The figure's reaction remained subdued, leaning back against the wall to take in my entire form. While this figure remained calm, others surrounding us growled and angrily murmured. That sulfur smell gained strength as I felt a vibration rise through my feet. As I watched, the figure tried to calm the ruckus by raising his hand. No dice, this time. More than the closest onlookers reacted. Sulfur laced the air so much that I felt a light coating on my dry tongue. Vibrations grew as well, as I felt it through my feet and my seat on the bench, flowing up the wall along my backbone.

"Excuse me a moment," the man said as he broke our connection. He pushed away from me and stood. Rolling his shoulders back, I thought he screamed. Whatever he did, the blast knocked me from the bench. I shook my head. It took a minute to clear my senses and to realize that the vibrations stopped. I twisted my body, rising to prop myself against the wall, back tight against the cold wood and stone. My previously occupied spot, the bench, faded from my view and took a bit of the sulfur smell with it. As the air cleared, I drew a deep breath, then exhaled it slowly. My mouth still felt dry, so I coughed once. Perhaps with the way my tongue felt, I expected to see a yellow cloud.

Someone said that ghosts caused the air to grow cold. I felt hot, overwhelmed with a need to strip naked. My needs got overridden as two glowing people settled beside me on the floor. One had followed me and laughed. He'd settled to my left. On my right, the glowing figure had a curvaceous shape, suggesting a shapely woman, but I couldn't be certain. Her hair color, her eye color, her skin color, even her scent. Nothing of this woman looked obvious beyond her curves, thanks to the yellow, shimmering light about her. Both figures sank a hand into my thigh.

"Oh, this one is Cute! Can I play with him?" Her voice sounded sultry, in a good middle register, with a slight hint of a rasp. I turned, looked into her eyes, and felt her hand slide along my thigh toward my waist.

"Not now, Maretta," the man said. His voice spoke with disgust and situation control, even with that simple, three-word sentence.

"You're no fun, Greg." Her lips formed a pout.

"I'll remind you of that uttered statement later." The feminine shimmer wiggled toward the other before she rolled away and faded through the floor. After watching this exit, I scanned the ranks of shimmering beings surrounding me. To my surprise, the ranks appeared thinned of their numbers compared with when I first fell here. Deciding my safest harbor sat beside me, I brought my gaze back to him and his face.

"Maretta? Maretta Stokes?" I waited for any acknowledgment. "Maretta was the last resident of unit three-twelve. She died of complications from a heart attack at age fifty-two. Paramedics declared her dead at her apartment. From my research before purchase, I found only one Maretta that lived in the building." Pondering this shimmering being, I searched through my memory. "The building's history of unnatural deaths listed two with the name Greg. One lived on the third floor, Greg Dynmore. The second one lived on the terrace level, Greg Janis. Both died of gunshot wounds, three years apart. From what I remember, only two people named Greg occupied any space within the building."

My conversation partner, Greg, moved so his feet pressed against the wall. His hand slid down to my calf as he looked at me. "You've done your homework well. I am the latter Greg." Laughing, he tilted his head at my calf. "I'd shake, except it would cut our communication."

I glanced at our connection, slid my eyes along the arm and torso of the being. "I see no gunshot wound."

Greg shook his head. "This isn't my physical being. It's not even my soul. This form is the physical manifestation of my life energy within this building."

Leaning forward, I placed my hands on my knees. "That means that you aren't technically here. No one, technically, lives here. You'll fade in time."

Greg shook his head a second time. "Those that needed to fade have already faded. Those of us that remain will stay while the building stands."

Staring at Greg, I tried to absorb all this information he'd thrown at me, especially regarding my investment. "I don't understand. Why does your group remain? Unfinished business? Not allowed to leave by someone holding you here?"

It shocked me, but I watched Greg draw a breath, then exhale it. "Your thoughts remain centered on soul, or spirit." He paused, looked at the balcony, then eyed the stairs. "Let me offer this thought. A person leaves a psychic impression on a room from their presence. The longer they stay, the greater the impression. If someone just passes through a room, it causes a slight wave. Living, existing in the room, imprints a much stronger energy. We exist because of that very imprint."

I shifted my body some to keep my hips from falling asleep. "So your energy imprinted ... the entire building?"

Greg laughed before he spoke. "I exist best within the rooms of my apartment, but because I made this building my home, stopping to talk, congregate, I travel the paths of the building as easily."

Absorbing all the information that this Greg had given me, I pondered the room, the space that I sat. "What about me? Am I creating a psychic imprint right now? How did the bench appear?"

Greg paused, considered the wall and floor. "Know what? I'm not entirely sure I know the details regarding the bench. It has something to do with psychic energy being able to manipulate surroundings within their internal experiences. Nigel knows more about it, having taught psychology for many years at a local community college."

"Our local college attendees still refer to a long retired professor as Nutty Nigel." That's when I looked around to find us almost alone. "Where did everyone else go?"

"Like most of living beings, once the initial excitement ends, they fade into the woodwork." Greg shrugged. "Most likely, if we traverse the halls, we'll meet someone."

As we sat talking, I realized something nagged my thoughts. "Didn't the Spirit Patrol attempt to cleanse this building?"

Greg made a soft snort as he shook his head. "Spirit Patrol. Yeah. They've tried. But because they had no psychics on staff, they didn't understand what we were and declared us evil energy beings. That's why they sealed the building. They've not visited in recent memory. I'm sure they've picked up a few new tricks since they harassed me and my neighbors."

Shrugging, I let my thoughts about revamping the building return. "Always considered the fools as charlatans, myself. They thrive on ripping the hard-earned dollar from the honest, unassuming consumer."

"Don't believe in spooks, ghosts, or others things that scare people, eh?" Greg said with a chuckle.

"My mind started changing once I met your lot," I said. Considering my college degree and the formal training built into my upbringing, the stories of ghosts, goblins, and spooks never made it to my ears. Not even a decent horror movie. Those stories I heard, the family and teachers dissected for the symbology and their elements of fiction. Removed all the fun from them. However, the reason they got written, to frighten and teach about the bad things, never connected with me. "Intellect has this downfall of removing the interest and fear inherent in a subject, by reducing it to something easy to dismiss."

Greg's chuckle grew to a laugh, drawing from deep within him for a belly shaking quake that even got me chuckling. "Do you work for our local community college now? That sounded like a Nigel commentary."

I shook my head and gestured to the building. "I'm a business person, trying to build an empire, one brick at a time. This building, I'd determined to make brick number two of my empire." Dropping my gaze to the tile floor that lined the entrance, I frowned. "It seemed like a grand plan, to revitalize this building and make it worth more than an abandoned historic landmark."

"Your plan will work," Greg said. "The existing residents won't enjoy their paths disrupted. However, if we work together, I think we could probably keep both your future tenants and my fellow psychic energy beings pleased." This statement drew my interest.

"What might this idea require?" We considered each other for a silent minute.

"I suspect I can explain better from your new gym." He gathered himself away from me and stood. Following his example, I climbed to my feet. My muscles objected after I'd not moved during our conversation. I'd not noticed the passage of time. Greg and I turned and mounted the stairs.

Walking up the stairs, I watched for damage and other possible necessary repairs. Each step needed new carpeting, but that didn't surprise me. Damage liked to hide beneath things like old carpet, so I didn't completely write off the solidity of the steps. The banister looked like it needed sanding, possibly a deep cherry stain, but its wood felt solid. Code might require adding extra supports, unless we got a historic building waiver. We paused on the landing and I stomped my feet. Solid wood echoed back. A shimmering man slid from beneath the landing and scowled at me. Greg placed his hand against my elbow.

"Elmer liked the closet beneath the stairs." He gestured to the man half through the floor. "No one understood why. Stomping on the landing meant stomping on his head, so I don't recommend it."

I glanced at the man. "Sorry, Elmer. Just making sure your ceiling remained solid." Blinking, Elmer slid back through the floor. Turning, I opened my mouth to ask Greg about Elmer. He shook his head.

"Elmer was the manager's son. Even after his family moved across town, Elmer came back to his closet. No one understood why." Pulling his hand away, Greg continued up the stairs, so I followed. My mental records said nothing about any of the building managers having a family, especially not a son. I'd have to research that fact when I got a chance.

When we reached the balcony, Greg glided to the railing and perched on the wood. I took my place beside him. We gazed across the empty lobby and I realized it remained almost pristine, with only a few minor repairs required. Offering a historic feel, it could have the selling point of nostalgia. When I turned to look at Greg, he smiled and nodded.

"Blueprints and plans never give a full feel of a building. One must walk its halls to appreciate what the building offers."

I nodded. "Now that I look at the interior, I can see adjusting my plans for the building's remodel. This perspective offered me an idea."

"As I hoped it might."

Gesturing toward the mailboxes, I turned to ask Greg about how the previous owners lit the lobby. The door shook, which shook the building. It rattled as someone slammed a solid object against it. From my perspective, I feared a dented steel door. I focused my attention toward the battering sound. Greg seemed to understand my concern as he waved his hand through the air.

With the next strike, the lock released, and the door bounced against the frame. The bounce kept it off the frame and created a small crack. Hands grabbed at the metal and pulled on it. Not willing to just give them free passage, Greg made them struggle to open the door enough for someone to enter. Once they had the space, we had guests.

Three people rushed through the opening, though none disturbed the tile as I had. Each person wore a polo shirt that had the Spirit Patrol logo stitched on the left breast pocket. A robust woman limped to the central position. Two men, one red-haired and the other black, positioned themselves to cover the flanks. All three held their hands before their chests in a type of ward. My original greeting party floated into the foyer and filled it, standing back from the three new people. After a quick glance toward Greg, I walked down the stairs. I reached the bottom and glanced behind me, only to watch Greg slid through the floor. Not wanting to startle the new arrivals, I eased two steps from the stairs, then paused. Maretta and Greg joined me.

The outside light haloed a new person entering the building. The bright light made me blink, and I smiled as my nervous business partner stood behind the wall of human spirit patrol shields.

After my extended conversation, I felt more in-tune with the shimmering people gathered around me. That meant I needed to act as liaison for them. My approach would dictate the reactions of all these new arrivals.

I made sure I didn't walk through the residents as I approached what I considered the battle line. Maretta drifted at my side, though I wasn't sure about her intentions. I slid past the closet line of my new friends and stood just a foot from the robust woman. Staring into her eyes, I noted she never blinked. My mind wandered to thoughts of her having dry lenses and needing some eye drops. It made me chuckle.

When I made my noise, she moved, her hands creating an elaborate design in the air before her. As she completed her design, she pushed the air where it was supposed to be floating. I felt nothing, saw nothing, and had no obvious reaction to it. The shimmering people behind me also didn't react. Maretta's hand slid into mine, and I heard yawns and snorts of derision from the others in the crowd. Smiling, I moved my attention to my partner.

"Does this mean that you've changed your mind?" I said. He flinched as I spoke. His eyes searched the room, but his gaze darted past me. Turning, I gave Maretta a questioning look. Her eyes widened a moment, then she released my hand. I took another two steps forward before my partner saw me.

"When did you learn to throw your voice?" he said. Dashing forward, he pushed past the spirit patrol members and threw his arms around me. "You're in one piece. Great. The evil spirits haven't shredded your essence yet."

I don't know why, but I grabbed my stomach and released a belly laugh. My partner drew back from me, his eyes widening. His hands gripped my upper arms, tight enough I felt my fingers develop a tingle.

"They aren't evil spirits. They claim that they're psychological essences of those who lived here. There is nothing evil about them, other than wanting to protect their homes."

"I'm being serious, and you're laughing and making up jokes." He tightened his grip and shook me. "Wake up, man! You're in trouble. In fact, we both are, the longer we stand here."

Greg stood behind me, placing his hand on my shoulder. "Anything I can do?" Greg's voice sounded calm, yet held a commanding tone. I never questioned why Greg's touch allowed me to remain visible, while Maretta's touch didn't.

With the physical contact, my partner must have heard Greg. He released my arms as he stumbled toward the spirit patrol. The woman who'd cast the protective design caught him, handed him to another member of the patrol. Then she turned to me, stepping into my personal space. Our noses almost touched. The smell wasn't as pleasant as I'd have hoped, though the sulfur started building to block out the other smell. I felt Greg snort.

"She's the one who declared us evil and uncooperative," Greg said. I offered a slight nod, but nothing else. The woman ran a hand over my left arm, frowned, then repeated the gesture. I felt tingles from her touch, but not much else.

"I'm Arian Smith, local Spirit Patrol commander," she said. "You're standing in the presence of evil entities. We couldn't confine them or eliminate them. By breaching our seal, you've released these entities and placed everyone at risk."

We stood and stared at each other, while Greg hovered behind me. When I didn't react, Arian pushed past me, waving her hands through the air. Her motions got her nowhere near Greg or his brethren. Some laughed at the motions, while others crossed their arms. Two of the lighted men moved to circle the spirit patrol members, dancing around and making faces at each member.

Only one spirit patrol member moved with them, watched them moving. This young lady seemed most ready to confront what she faced, though also possibly a low ranked member whom the leadership might ignore. While I wanted to approach her, I knew I had a different destination. I walked to Arian's side, where I touched her elbow. I thought I'd made my approach obvious, but Arian still flinched when I made contact. Greg walked to us and placed his hand against the connection between Arian and me.

"I'm not sure what you're planning, but we tried talking to her last time," Greg said. "It didn't work." Arian's head whipped around to stare at me.

"You've put voices in my head," she said. I felt her voice's venom.

"I'm doing no such thing. Instead, I'm suggesting that your team work with a more open mind. We're not in danger here."

"Bull. This happened last time. We heard voices, but we found no one. Evil lives here."

"I told you so," Greg said. I glared at Greg, then addressed Arian again.

"How much research did your outfit do before attempting to cleanse the building?" My question threw Arian, because she stared at me with these wide eyes.

"Research? We get a call and we try to cleanse the building. No research goes into our work."

I looked at Greg and nodded. He shrugged before he walked away to check another grouping in the room. "Then perhaps your firm needs to change its procedure," I said. With a wide gesture that encompassed the room, I smiled. "We're not in danger, because these people just wanted to protect their homes. They aren't demons, devils, or evil spawn." My gesture brought a smile to the face of one patrol member, as they moved toward one lighted being. I caught a connection and a conversation. Greg didn't touch me, so I couldn't hear the conversation, but I thought it must come across as positive. Both laughed. Pointing toward the woman who followed my new friends, I chuckled, but couldn't continue to speak. Arian took my attitude as an insult, throwing her hands against me and shoving me into a pillar.

"No mere man could dictate how our patrol operates," she said with a bellow. Again, she created some sign in the air. Then she threw it at me. Nothing happened. I laughed. Stepping from the pillar, I gestured to Greg.

"On your team, you've got someone who sees these beings," I said. "Has anyone asked her about this situation?"

Without waiting for her to react, I walked to the young woman and touched her shoulder. The nearest shimmery figure touched the opposite shoulder. This started a chain reaction of connections between living and shimmers. Greg placed his hand on mine. Arian came to our side, eyes wide from shock but realization. When I looked, I saw Greg touch Arian's shoulder with his other hand, creating a full chain among us. Standing on the room's edge, I heard all the conversations that people shared. One patrol member commented that he'd spoken with one projection's relative. My eyes locked on Arian, watching her search the room and find the conversations. Understanding grew and her face relaxed. With Greg and Arian clearing the misunderstanding between them, I left to find my partner.

I pulled myself from my little gathering, allowing Greg to complete the circuit without me, then walked toward the exit. My hands remained shoved in my pockets, so I didn't feel tempted to find out what the group discussed. More patrol members created a wide barrier around the door. No one tried to stop me as I left the building. Outside, I held my hand to shield my eyes from the bright sun. It rested just above the buildings, so I'd spend most of the afternoon within the building negotiating with Greg and his friends. Seated on his car's hood, I saw my partner, his arms wrapped around his stomach. He rocked forward and back as he stared at his feet. Three large passenger vans sat in the parking lot behind his car, along with one converted miniature school bus. Inside the bus, two people worked their electronic devices, but they seemed especially occupied.

The short distance felt longer as I walked to my partner. I slipped onto the hood next to him, marveled that the metal felt warm still. We sat in silence for two minutes. Then my partner surprised me when he turned and threw his arms around my shoulders.

"Thank all that's holy you're alive," he said in a gush. Shoving against his chest, I pulled myself out of his embrace.

"The problem wasn't dangerous, unless we consider miscommunication dangerous." We fell into silence again. My eyes traveled the sidewalk, searched the grounds around the building. When they returned to the entrance door, I saw the spirit patrol officers stepping from within the building. Some laughed and others shook their heads. "While I was inside, the residents offered ideas on how to renovate the place. It won't require a complete gut and rebuild. We'll need to bring things to code, but we won't need to decimate the original feel of the building."

"You being serious? Ghosts gave you ideas about how to fix the building. I'm in shock."

"Sarcasm doesn't suit your personality," I said with a sigh. "Come inside and meet them."

"I don't want to suffer the same brainwashing." Pulling himself off the hood, he brushed his pants. "My lawyer will contact yours about the contract."

Slipping from the hood, I let him walk past and climb into the driver's side. The engine roared as he started the car. Just before he pulled away, he glanced over at me and shook his head. His tires left rubber stripes on the asphalt when he peeled out of the parking lot. I continued to stand and wait, watched the first two passenger vans reload with the spirit patrol members. They left at a more leisurely pace, with each heading a different direction.

Arian left the building last, though she stopped and removed the patrol's sticker. She talked to someone as she walked along the sidewalk. I couldn't see who. As a guess, Greg might have walked with her. I didn't know if any previous resident had that ability.

Then I thought about it. Of course they could leave. They walked to the parking lot just like they walked the building's halls. The sun would just prevent their usual glow from appearing. The residents might have continued to follow routines with no one realizing it.

Walking the length of the sidewalk, Arian paused when she reached me and I felt a presence beside me. A hand settled on my shoulder, then I heard other voices.

"Thank you for helping to open our eyes," Arian said. "Were it not for this revelation, we would have forgotten our true purpose. And missed a more open mind among us without meaning to."

I shrugged. "Sometimes, the most open-minded people encounter the greatest blocks when something new appears." My gaze drifted back to the building. "Though it sometimes takes new information to fully understand how complicated life is."

Arian laughed, clapped my shoulder, then walked toward the last van. She climbed into the driver's seat. Hands waved from open windows as the van left the parking lot.

"We've made new friends, possibly the first of our tenants." Greg spoke through the shoulder link, but I couldn't see him. It didn't matter. "The leader worked with her staff member to find the proper channel and we can move forward safely. Building restoration will become our primary task."

Greg and I returned to the building, discussing our plans and preparing for the next era of tenants.

The Haunting of a Guard

The gunshots echoed in his ear.

Christian lowered his gun, looked across the courtyard, and saw the prisoner lying in a puddle of his own blood. The puddle didn't stick around long as the parched ground swallowed it. A small dust cloud hovered over the fallen body.

Allowing the rifle's barrel to hit the dirt, Christian blinked. Did his shot kill the convict? He stood on the line's end and he'd only passed his shooting ability test by single digits. Someone else must have killed him. Or did they? He couldn't be sure. He'd closed his eyes and turned his head when he pulled the trigger. His gaze slid left as he examined the other four members of the firing squad. One guard smiled and nodded while another fidgeted with the slide on his rifle. The last two stared at Guard Captain Rostoff, their guns hanging by their sides, barely within their fingers.

Stepping forward from behind the line, Guard Captain Rostoff strutted across the courtyard. In his dress blues, he presented the image of a rooster or a peacock. He approached the body, walked to either side as he gazed at the prisoner's chest. As he saw no movement, he knelt beside the body and pressed his fingers against the man's neck. Christian's heart pounded in his chest. After a minute passed, Captain Rostoff nodded and stood.

"Good job, men. Successful execution." The Guard Captain pivoted on his heels. "Dismissed!" His ultimate command echoed about the silent courtyard as the gunshots had. With another parade ground twist, the Guard Captain strutted through the courtyard and departed through its far door.

Christian heard two guards celebrate, but he didn't feel the same glee. Neither did his stomach. His legs wobbled while his tongue passed over parched lips. He kept gazing at the body. When he raised his focus to the courtyard's wall, he saw the dead convict standing there, holding his hands away from his sides. It didn't look like the prisoner they had just killed. No, this person stood without a blindfold. And his jumpsuit looked clean and new.

Christian rubbed his eyes and his vision cleared. Well, it cleared of everything except the body, its faded puddle, and a blood streak on the courtyard's dull stone wall. He hadn't paid attention to the streak before, as the dead man concerned him more. Not like that mattered. The convict had died by a firing squad, as the judge ordered.

After shouldering his rifle, Christian turned on his heels and walked to the staff gate. Another guard opened the gate, slapped Christian on the shoulder as he passed. If he said something, Christian missed it.

Christian hated executions. He'd avoided that part of his duty for three months. Until today. The thought of killing someone, even if the criminal deserved it, created an uncomfortable image for him. Somehow, unclean just didn't describe it. That felt too simple. Trying to shake off the disturbing thoughts, he walked along the hall and turned the corner for the guards' break room. He stopped when he saw what waited for him.

The dead convict stood in the hall with his hands spread from his sides and five bullet holes in his chest. Crimson blood flowed from the holes and down the prisoner's dusty jumpsuit. Around his feet, more blood created a puddle on the floor. As the image reached out to Christian, a hand closed over his shoulder.

Christian screamed. He backpedaled until he slammed himself against the wall.

"Easy there, pal-oh," Brandon said. He was another guard from Christian's training class and had just walked around the corner.

Pulling himself away from the wall, Christian looked down the hall. The image had vanished. His eyes were playing tricks on him, kept him on edge. He turned his head and tried to smile at Brandon. The fake expression worked, it appeared. Brandon nodded.

"Your first execution, eh?" Brandon patted Christian's shoulder. "My first here, but fourth overall. They get easier from here. Let's get you a drink to calm your nerves."

They walked down the short hallway to the break room door. Brandon pushed it open and held it. Glancing through the doorway, Christian searched for any sign of the dead man. He didn't see him. In fact, the room appeared deserted. They walked through the door and crossed to the small wooden bar built of pallets and storage crates. Supervisors had posted a sign above the bar. The sign warned everyone that only executioners could use this bar. And they could only use it after said executions happened.

Brandon slipped behind the bar, jostled through the stored liquor, and drew a small square bottle from within it. The whiskey sloshed as he pulled out the stopper. He filled two small glasses, replaced the stopper in the bottle, and dropped it beneath the bar. One glass he pushed into Christian's hand while he raised the other glass to shoulder height.

"To another successful kill. May all deaths be as quick and painless."

Christian raised his glass. It hovered inches from his lips. His free hand rose to cover his ear. The gunshot rang in his ear again. His eyes closed a moment but, when they opened, he couldn't believe what he saw. The whiskey looked deep red, like the color of blood. That couldn't be right. He drew the glass close until it touched his nose's tip and gazed into the contents. No denying it. Colored red like fresh-drawn blood and smelled like it, too. Something rolled across the glass's bottom. It didn't clink on the glass like an ice cube. Because he didn't recall Brandon putting ice cubes into the glass, Christian turned his head to get a better assessment of the liquid. He dropped the glass onto the bar and stumbled backwards, where he tripped over a chair. After falling onto his butt, he pointed at the glass.

"Why did you pour me a glass of blood? With an eyeball?" His finger wavered, though he didn't know why shivers flowed over him. Brandon grabbed the glass off the bar and frowned into it.

"I didn't. It's whiskey." Bringing the glass to his lips, Brandon took a small sip. "See? Good, strong alcohol designed to calm your nerves." Pushing himself back to his feet, Christian approached the bar. The whiskey had returned to a transparent orange-red color, unlike blood. He dipped a finger into the glass's contents and brought it to his lips. After tasting the glass's contents, he nodded. He grabbed the glass and dumped the contents into his mouth, swallowing it all in one gulp. It burned his throat as it coated its way down, forced him to focus on the present, existing pain. The glass landed lightly on the bar. Brandon refilled it. Christian emptied it in one gulp a second time, wiping his mouth with his sleeve as he set the glass down. When Brandon raised the bottle, Christian waved him away.

"I'm going to talk to the captain." The whiskey hadn't gotten to him, he thought, but he still stumbled toward the door. When he reached the doorframe, he grabbed it to steady himself and pull himself around the corner, toward the end of the hall. A gunshot echoed through his head. His eyes swept the hall, but he saw no one with a gun. In fact, he saw no one. He stumbled the fifteen feet to the captain's office door. Light shone through the small, frosted glass window. Christian thought he saw the captain sitting at his desk. Christian's hand reached for the doorknob, but he stopped it before he touched the metal.

Blood oozed around the upper doorframe and flowed over the door's wood surface. It covered the door's upper third, stopping at the window's edge. While Christian watched, a puddle of blood formed along the edge of the window, growing with each passing moment. A single drip broke from the puddle to dribble across the frosted window, with a bullet leading the river of red ooze down the smooth surface. As he stared, he got the taste of dust in his mouth. It reminded him of the dust from the courtyard, from when he broke apart two scuffling inmates. That dust had ground into his teeth for weeks. One of those inmates he just shot. Another gunshot rumbled through his head and the blood flow seemed to double.

Unable to take anything else, Christian turned around and ran, screaming, down the hall. At the hall junction, he turned and headed deeper into the facility. He kept running until he tripped over a mop and fell into Charlie, the head janitor. Mop water splashed across Christian's uniform pants. The water soaked his uniform from his knees to his boots. It created a crust made of the courtyard dust.

Christian gathered himself back onto his feet and placed one hand against the wall to steady himself. Charlie squeezed his mop out into the half empty bucket, then pressed the mop against the puddle at Christian's feet.

"What's the problem, fella?" Having worked at the facility for twenty-five years, Charlie had heard it all and seen it all. He acted like the guards' uncle. He'd offered his support for things they couldn't explain to the captain.

Christian leaned over and grabbed his knees as he drew a few deep breaths. He watched the mop taking the water and mud away from the floor about his feet. The water remained water, and it didn't shift to blood. For the first minute, he felt like he'd approached his old self. Pulling himself upright, Christian leaned against the wall.

"I think I shot someone."

"That's a part of your job. Most guards like you that can't handle it, they get stinking drunk afterward. Or so I hear," Charlie said. He stepped closer and sniffed Christian's breath. "I think you'll require more drink to bury these memories in your case." He stepped back and dunked the mop head into the bucket again.

With a shake of his head, Christian threw his hands around with wild gestures. "I'm seeing the dead man everywhere. If I don't see him, I see his blood, my bullet. I taste the dust of the courtyard, taste and smell his blood. No matter what I try, I can't get away from them."

Charlie nodded as he wrung out the mop, dropped it onto the stone floor. He cleaned a small square of the floor. After a minute, he folded his hands atop the mop handle and looked at Christian. His mouth opened, thought better of it, then closed his mouth. Christian wondered what Charlie considered saying, what he knew. In other conversations, the custodian never hesitated. The mop cleaned another square of the floor before Charlie stopped a second time. He folded his hands around the end of the mop, gazed at Christian. Christian felt Charlie's eyes as they scaled his face, measuring his soul. Taking a hand from the mop, Charlie grasped Christian's arm.

"The images fade, son. Get drunk, sleep the drink off, and you'll be fine." He pushed the mop into the bucket. The move slid the bucket against the wall and opened a passage for Christian.

Calmed but not convinced, Christian shuffled through the opening. At his slower pace, it took him ten minutes to reach the stairs leading to the bunk room. He placed his hand against the wall, raised his foot to mount the first step. It felt like his foot missed the step, falling to the flat of the hall floor. Dust rose from the ground where his foot landed and it coated his clothes. It rose until it filled his mouth, his nose. Christian coughed as he tried to clear the courtyard dust from his mouth. With his second cough, he noticed a secondary flavor to the dust. A metallic tang mingled with the grit. His fingers dug into the wall. Using that leverage, he pulled himself onto the steps. He ran the flight, gaining distance two steps at a time.

Christian reached the top, stopped, and caught his breath. Sunlight streamed through a west-facing window. Birds darted between the rooftops of the various prison buildings. Their songs drifted on the small breezes that moved the room's air. It created such a cheerful scene, one that Christian couldn't absorb. After stomping his feet at the top stair landing, Christian turned and stumbled to his bunk, the fourth from the door. He dropped face first onto the flat surface, face-first into the pillow. He dragged himself over until he stretched the full length of the bed. The darkness filled his vision for but a minute before the courtyard scene returned. A continuous reel of film, it played without end across his vision, throughout his thoughts. When the fifth cycle began, he sat upright on his bunk. His hands grabbed his temples as his elbows fell onto his knees.

Christian decided Brandon and Charlie must know something. Both advised him to get stinking drunk. One drink had spiraled his thoughts in too many unpleasant directions, ones he didn't want to follow. After taking a minute to rub his temples, he stood and walked to his footlocker. A swift kick against its side and the top popped open. He knelt. His hand reached into the open space. Shifting a spare blanket to the side, he uncovered a large bottle of bourbon and a pistol, both items nestled among his clothes. He'd received the bourbon as a gift from his proud uncle, who'd served four tours in the military. Christian had taken one shot, then stashed the rest.

His hands grabbed either side of the footlocker as he sat on his heels. The echo of another gunshot filled his head as the taste of the courtyard's bloody dust filled his mouth. Blood oozed over the hinges and puddled in the footlocker's lid. As he closed his eyes, Christian shook his head. Even with his eyes closed, he saw the dead prisoner, with confusion lacing his facial features. The man's blood dripped into Christian's open footlocker. Without opening his eyes, Christian reached into the footlocker.

GUARD CAPTAIN ROSTOFF climbed the steps to the bunk room. One of his guards had disappeared, and the captain needed to find him. He had feared the boy wasn't ready for the firing line, but he followed his old commander's orders. Get the raw recruits onto the firing line early and often. Placed on the far end, the young guard's shot had no chance of striking the criminal. His shooting ability needed to improve. It gave the boy situational experience, however, so he could develop the callous it required. To do it right, each guard needed to adjust to the job. This young guard hadn't had time. And now the Guard Captain had to search for his wayward guard. That didn't settle the captain's mind well.

This guard, Christian, missed the start of his shift. His other guards had a scuffle among prisoners to settle, so Captain Rostoff went searching for his missing guard. Most of the guards, wanting to forget the firing squad's events, got drunk, then returned to their bunks. Many slept the day, though none missed a shift. Captain Rostoff hoped that was the situation here.

As he reached the landing, his eyes surveyed the bunk room. Lots of empty bunks, so the floor became the next logical spot. He spotted the boy stretched out beside his footlocker. Perhaps he'd gotten so blackout drunk he couldn't make it into his bunk. It had happened before. It wouldn't surprise him to happen again. His body position didn't suggest someone who'd fallen asleep where they lay. Even a drunk one.

As a trained soldier and military police person, Captain Rostoff passed through the door and walked closer, then stopped. He'd treat it as a crime scene. He sighed as he settled onto the footlocker beside the boy's bunk. His attention locked on the scene about him. He couldn't tear his gaze from the pistol in the boy's hand, the hole in the boy's head, or the puddle of blood around his shoulders. It wouldn't require medical training for him to know that his missing guard was dead. As he sat and stared, he heard someone come up the stairs. Rostoff heard the bucket creak as Charlie walked across the short section of floor and stood near him. Both men groaned softly. Charlie's hand settled onto Captain Rostoff's shoulder.

"He wasn't ready," Captain Rostoff said. Charlie tightened his grip.

Soul Explorations

The funeral home stood in a quieter part of town. Its two-story, white brick building had a manicured lawn, appeared unassuming when compared with its similar neighbors. Within the funeral home, Janet and her two companions stood behind the casket. Janet had attended funerals for friends, but she didn't enjoy being the focus. She didn't want to stand here, but her new friends, Percy and Jerome, had insisted. The home's staff had closed the casket so the mourners couldn't see her body. If she considered how she'd died, their decision was a good thing.

Her companions surveyed the gathering while standing within the semicircle of brightly colored irises. The funeral home staff used flowers to separate the caskets from the rest of the room. Clusters of people stood talking, smiling, and hugging. It created a cheery scene as they greeted their fellow mourners. Each cluster shifted and reformed as people peeled off one to join others. New arrivals wove through the various groups, pausing for quick greetings before approaching the casket. One or two cried when they arrived. Sister Bernice hummed Amazing Grace. Off key as usual, since no one had the heart to tell her.

No one noticed Janet and her two companions. But their focus wasn't on them. After giving themselves time to say their goodbyes, people drifted away to join their groups and gathered in more supporting arms. Outside the semicircular flower ring near the casket, the room felt like a lighthearted occasion.

"Mine wasn't anything like this," Percy said under his breath. "The women all bawled and wailed. Tissues filled a corner of the room. The cleaning crew said they couldn't find the wastebasket when everyone left."

"Be thankful people came to your funeral," Jerome said. "Mine had only my immediate family and even they complained about attending. My youngest didn't even bother to show." He drifted from behind the casket and traveled around the flower's outer edge. He sighed and looked at the ceiling. His walk brought him back behind the casket. Because her two companions weren't paying attention, Janet walked around the casket, around her dead body.

"I want to join them," Janet said. "I want to mingle with them, comfort them." Taking a step forward, she slid between two flowerpots. Percy and Jerome scrambled to catch her. They jumped the flowers and grabbed her under her arms as she got two steps beyond the pots. The room's energy chilled while the three stood beyond the flowers. Bodily, they dragged her back within the semicircle.

"You can't," Percy said. "To them, we're gone." They released her arms, but Percy stood in front of her. She feigned trying to dash around him, but Percy moved with her, kept her back.

"If any of us stepped beyond the flowers, it would change the room's mood," Jerome said. "We don't want to disrupt that growing, happy feeling. Do we?"

Janet paused. Her gaze traveled between the two men and the rest of the gathering. Her family and friends gathered beyond the flowers. Beyond her reach. She felt more from their presence now than she had when she lived. They spoke about their joys of her nearness when she lived. One couple discussed their lost opportunities to others, regarding books and other gatherings. Her left foot tried to slide between the flowers. Percy tapped it. As she felt the rebuke, she pulled herself back. She tried moving to a different location among the flowerpots, but she heard more of the same discussions. Some internal drive kept pulling her out toward her friends, but she shook her head and stepped behind the casket.

"How?" Janet asked. Turning her back on the mourners, she directed her entire attention toward the two men. "How does anyone do this? I mean watching as they gather, as they say goodbye. This can't be easy."

Jerome shrugged as he ran his hand along the casket's lid. "It gets easier as time passes. I think I'll make this funeral my last one, though."

Percy frowned, as he lowered his chin and shook his head. He said nothing. Janet placed her hand on Jerome's shoulder.

Jerome flinched at the touch, looked at the ceiling, and sighed. "Everyone will forget in time. This casket and every other one out there will become some future archeologist's prized finds." He raised his hands in mock surprise. "Check out what this society has done with their dead!"

"Oh, come on, quit it," Percy said, as he grasped the man's shoulders. "You're going to bring down the room's mood. It's as bad as her walking beyond the flowers." He turned to Janet. "He gets like this toward the end every single time. It's something about being forgotten."

Their group settled into silent observation as the rest of the visitation hours passed. Toward the end, the facility's director walked into the room. They wove through the crowd and approached the casket. Stopped in front of the irises, the director folded their hands. To move people along, the director guided the crowd toward the door. People drifted toward the room's rear and the crowd thinned. Janet watched the thinning crowd, eyeing the door and counting as people left. It dwindled down to her immediate family. Her husband stood beside the couch along the wall and her middle daughter sat next to him, sobbing, and held a picture to her chest. Based on the frame, the picture came from when the family stood together as the youngest daughter got her driver's license. Her older son remained in Europe with the military and couldn't get home, while her youngest daughter hid in the bathroom. That left these two.

"So, what do I do now?" Janet walked around the casket, her hand resting lightly on the lid. "I can't exactly go to work like this."

Jerome and Percy looked at each other. Then they laughed.

"We try to move beyond our mortal bounds," Percy said. "This is our way. Some of us stay behind to help others with the transition, but we're a sparsely populated group." Percy poked his thumb toward Jerome. The man stuck his tongue out at Percy. "This old timer doesn't seem to want to leave." He gently nudged Jerome in the ribs. "Popular gossip suggests it's because he wants to know what it's like to have people like him."

Jerome snorted. "Bull Hockey."

"How do I join the transition team?" Janet found herself distracted as her family spoke with the funeral home staff. However, her attention returned to Jerome and Percy.

Percy shrugged. "Just stick around. That's all we did."

"Yeah, just stick around. People will mistake you for being a caring soul." Jerome moved to the wall, sitting against it so he could run his fingers through the flowers. His mood seemed to darken from the contact. Grumbling, he rolled backward and through the wall.

Janet blinked. "That's a new trick," she said. She turned and smiled at Percy. "Can we all do that?"

"With practice," Percy said. "Let me offer something back closer to our old topic. We don't know when death will happen. Not any more than when we lived. Those of us who've stayed, we just act as guides to help with understanding and the next steps."

"That's a lot to take in. All these new experiences take a lot to absorb."

"Which is why we have guides."

"Is someone, maybe someone new like me, allowed to guide?"

"You'd never do this alone. We're always a tag team to help the new arrivals."

Janet thought she knew her choice, but her mind waffled between walking away and maybe staying. Oh, she didn't know. Janet drifted up to the ring of flowers. They got her favorite flower in her favorite color. Her fingers passed through the petals of a bearded iris as Jerome jumped into view, floating down from the ceiling.

"Hey! They have a teen viewing upstairs in two hours," Jerome said. "From what I saw in her casket, she got mashed in a car accident."

"You are too happy for a dead teenager, Jerome," Percy said as he frowned. "Especially around our other new arrival." Of course, Percy meant her, but it still made Janet feel a little self-conscious.

Jerome crossed his arms and pouted. "I gotta find my kicks somewhere, don't I?"

As she listened to the two men, Janet examined her own desires based on where she stood now. Her death hit her hard and quick. However, her life had many worthy memories. Even after her review, she thought she should step into this next life, whatever that life might hold. But she had work to complete in this life as well. Walking along the ring of flowers, she watched the last of her family leave the room. Her children waited out in the antechamber, just beyond the viewing room. With no one nearby, she wanted to get closer so she could hear better. Janet drifted toward the room's archway that separated it from the antechamber and hallway. She leaned against the wall. Final hugs passed between family and friends as the undertaker arrived at the door. The undertaker looked right at her. No, that couldn't be. He turned his back, blocking anyone from reentering the viewing room. It also blocked her view into the antechamber. Turning from the living, Janet strolled to the ring of flowers. Her two companions watched her, with each positioned at opposite ends of the casket.

"What do we do now?" Janet asked. "Are we stuck here? Forever?"

Percy shook his head. "No, we're free to return to the gathering point or to roam the world, helping others they encounter as they cross. Those that roam, if they get too far from known parts, lose their way. They create disturbances that then draw groups to hunt down and film. It gives both the living and the dead pleasure."

"What to do now? To be honest, that choice remains in the hands of the newest arrival." Jerome shrugged. "We choose to stick close to the funeral home and cemetery, along with a couple others, to help souls like yourself." Janet tried to absorb all that she'd learned. She'd not seen anyone else. Her knees felt weak. She sat on a bench by the wall.

"What's the gathering point?" She laced her fingers together and stared down at her shoes.

"It's the place to which all souls feel drawn. The light everyone talks about," Percy said. He and Jerome stayed by the casket, which Janet appreciated. The lack of incessant prattle helped, too.

"Does everyone feel like they haven't completed all their work when they reach this point?" She folded her hands in her lap and stared at the nails. They had gained the color that they'd painted the corpse's nails. It didn't match her blouse correctly. As she stared, the shade changed. Weird.

"Sometimes, when the person died early in life, they feel that way." Percy sat next to Janet. She'd not heard him approach. He placed a hand on her shoulder. "Perhaps we need a different perspective. Let's take a walk. It'll clear your head." Janet nodded and let Percy guide her to her feet. Jerome and Percy each took one of Janet's arms. They guided Janet into the antechamber when the undertaker strolled past the group and into the room.

"Evening, gents. Ma'am." A soft bass rumbled from the undertaker as he moved toward the casket.

"Hey, Douglas." Percy waved and Jerome nodded.

Janet froze with a gasp. "He can see us?"

The men laughed as the undertaker paused, moved his head to gaze at them. He smiled and nodded toward Janet, then continued his walk to the casket. Jerome gestured to the hallway and guided the trio as they walked toward the door. Janet turned once, looking at the undertaker as he pushed the casket's rolling cart from among the flowers. Her two guides retrieved her attention for their egress out. Once they stood outside the rooms, Percy explained.

"Anyone who works with human remains or who counsels the grieving, they can see the deceased's psychic projection, also called the soul by most people. It has something to do with their internal beliefs. I've not fully understood the whole thing. The stronger the person's beliefs, the more likely they will see the projection. Douglas has been around since before Jerome's funeral thirty-five years ago. So he has seen many of us." Gesturing toward the rear glass doors, he smiled. "Oh, look. It's sunny outside. That always helps. Let's check out to the rear parking lot."

As Percy and Janet walked toward the door, she noticed Jerome remained standing in the hallway. He gazed at the nearby stairwell. Janet paused, but Percy tugged on her arm to keep her moving. No comments passed among the three. At the door, she shifted her gaze to Jerome again. He waved his hand at her to continue, while he faded into the nearby wall. She tried not to gasp. Percy wrapped his hand around her elbow and guided her through the door. Literally. The doors didn't open, which sent a shudder through Janet. That part, she didn't think that she'd get used to doing.

Outside, they stood on the stoop, looking over the still emptying parking lot. People stood in small groups by their cars, chatting softly. As friends and family departed, they received a series of hugs from the others before they climbed into their car and drove away. The sun made everyone's mood appear brighter. Sunlight helped Janet see flows of energy she'd not noticed.

Percy touched her elbow, gestured away from the groups of people. They stepped from the stoop onto the sidewalk that took them around the parking lot's perimeter. The walk allowed Janet to see the energies from different angles. It surprised her when she saw energy bouncing back from a father as he stood beside his children. That explained what she'd seen between them when she was alive.

"Why don't people see how their reactions create such flows?"

"Some do," Percy said. "Some feel it more than they see it. Others remain oblivious, by choice, more than any other reason."

At the back left corner, Percy stopped. Janet's gaze never left the parking lot while they walked. She'd have kept going, had Percy not held her elbow still. When she felt the insistent tug, she turned to find that they stood near a mulch path leading into the trees. Bird song called to Janet, so she let Percy guide her away from the people and among the trees. This small patch of nature in the city made her feel more energized.

They stayed on the path for a short distance before they stepped onto the pine needle covered ground. Janet recognized the trees, the scents, the feel of the ground under her feet. She stood in the park near her childhood home. Blinking, she shook her head. That can't be right. Her gaze went to Percy as a frown developed on her face. Her childhood home had stood five states to the west of where they started. Rumor suggested that the house and this park had become the foundation for a large corporate building.

"How? Where?" Janet couldn't find the words for her questions.

"We just walked. Your thoughts brought us to where your mind felt most comfortable," he said with a smile. "Another part of this I don't fully understand. Perhaps it brought us to when your energy felt strongest. All I know is that you brought us here. This place, this time."

Still reeling from their travel, Janet stumbled for two steps, placing her hand against the tree. As she made contact, she understood the tree. The tree remembered her from childhood, when she scaled its trunk and curled in its branches, so she could read a book. No one had visited the tree since her family left. Janet's hand leapt from the tree as she twisted to gaze at Percy. He'd leaned against another tree, slipped his hands into his pockets.

"I understand why your thoughts brought us here now," he said. He closed his eyes as he pressed his shoulders against the rough bark. "The trees offer very soothing conversations."

"Trees talk?" Janet tried to sound calm, but she felt sure that her confusion caused her voice to fluctuate through different registers. "They're things," she said.

Percy opened his right eye. "Somehow, I don't think you've always had such an insulting opinion," he said with a chuckle. "After all, according to this tree, your childhood games had more open-minded play. Sometimes they included talking to the birds, the squirrels, the local opossum, the trees, the rocks, and anything else that would listen. Few people from your younger life would." His shoulders shifted as he tightened his left eye. "It says that your siblings taunted everyone not like them mercilessly, especially their youngest sister. Klutzy, non athletic, no creativity. They were brutal."

Both eyes opened as he pushed himself off the tree. His feet strode across the pine needles without disturbing them, though the smell of the fresh pine tickled Janet's nose. She closed her eyes and inhaled. Her head swam.

A memory brought her to a day when she curled in the branches of the tree, a can of peanuts hidden within one jacket pocket. She'd popped the nuts in her mouth as she read her book. After about ten minutes, a barking squirrel drew her attention. It stood on the tree's trunk, with its head toward her. Its tail flicked with each bark. Janet wondered why, so she looked around. Beyond her position, a few acorns hung from the branch.

Slipping her hand into her pocket, Janet grabbed a peanut and offered it to the squirrel. The squirrel dashed up the tree to another branch. At first, it barked at her again, but it stopped once it noticed the nut. Janet didn't move. In a show of bravery, the squirrel inched down the trunk, chittering as it moved. When it got close enough, it yanked the peanut from Janet's hand, then returned to its branch. Janet watched the squirrel shift the nut between its feet, looking it over. Then it bit into the nut, though it continued to turn it as it ate.

Janet laughed and returned to her book. She'd read a paragraph when she felt a tug on her coat. Her gaze shifted from the book to the fluffy tail poking out of her jacket pocket. The squirrel pulled its head from the can with puffed-out cheeks. It held a peanut in its feet as well. Realizing Janet had caught it, the squirrel darted up the tree. After that slight distraction, she read the next chapter and didn't dwell on the squirrel or the nuts for the rest of her time that she stayed within the tree.

The memory faded as Janet walked from the tree and toward the nearest clearing. She'd found it an enjoyable place to stretch out and stare at the stars on pleasant evenings. A quiet place to hide from her family when they started arguing. That silent refuge everyone sought but never found.

If they were really here, her park had changed since her family last lived in the area. It wasn't under a building, thankfully. Where there was once open space, they'd created a soccer field. Her field still existed, kind of, but fences and goals blocked the easy access the open spaces provided. The local department of parks locked the fences, so people couldn't just enter and enjoy as she had in her youth. Janet tried to not sigh in disgust at the urbanization of her park. She wanted to force trees to grow through the field.

Percy placed a hand on Janet's shoulder, which reminded her she didn't stand here alone. In her explorations, she'd almost forgotten he was there. Almost.

They walked to the gate in silence. Reaching out, Janet placed her hand on the lock. It didn't move to allow her to enter. Percy walked through the gate and stood by the nearest goal. With a shake of her head, Janet followed him through the fence. It sent tingles through her as the metal passed through her non corporeal body. She didn't think she'd ever get used to that. He grabbed the post, looked around the area. Then he turned back to Janet.

"This isn't what your early memories showed," he said. "This is more recent."

"Nothing remains the same, does it? Change and death are the only constants." This time, she kept herself from sighing, but it didn't change her overall feeling. Her reaction to many situations of late had been a sigh. That felt wrong.

"Does this mean you're still staying to help guide new souls?"

"I'm not sure." Walking away from the goal, she stopped at the center of the soccer pitch. "I might spend time here, exploring my old memories."

"You'll have a limited time for that pursuit, then they'll require the Decision." He paused. "The limit's five years, but that time goes faster than people expect, especially in our state."

Janet nodded. Walking across the pitch, she worked through the consequences of each of her decisions. They didn't sit well either way. She reached down and ran her fingers through the grass, watching as the blades passed through her fingers. When she concentrated, she felt the blades, soft and lush. The change to the soccer field had come recently. This grass still felt as it had when she'd spent her summer nights staring into the heavens, trying to decide which star she wanted to visit when she grew up.

"If I decide to stay, how do I state when I'm ready to leave?" She hadn't turned to find Percy near her. She knew he waited for her.

"Return to the funeral home," Percy said. "Follow the path we traveled to arrive here."

Janet heard him move, but couldn't tell where he went.

"We don't lose our ability to decide in this state, just how long it takes to make those decisions. Also, our choices still affect everything around us, so no matter what your decision is, something else will hinge on it, living or dead."

"I didn't realize I'd traveled with a philosopher," Janet said as she rose from her inspection. She rotated on her heels, but found she stood alone between two soccer goals. "Percy?"

A bat flew by, adjusting its flight to avoid her. No bugs approached her location, so that made sense. Instead, she discovered she had the same problem as she would when alive. Stuck with a major, life-altering decision and no one around to help her with it. Life-altering. She laughed.

Since she wanted to see where her memories took her, she felt it was time to explore the next one. She walked from the soccer pitch toward the park's outbuildings. Her travel changed the landscape, bringing with it a new field, a new period for her to explore.

When she took a step, she didn't stand within a memory, but in a present situation. Janet found herself outside a large college field house. Her daughter had her graduation robes draped over her arm as she scrambled across the grassy field. Students flowed toward the field house like lemmings to a cliff. Janet tried to think how long it had been since she'd died. Then she remembered Percy's comment regarding how time worked here. She thought her daughter didn't graduate from college for another month. Well, that was true when she died. Since her husband made it, since their daughter deserved the support that she could no longer give.

Curious, Janet followed the crowd into the field house. The wall proved no challenge for her to pass through. That came easier than she expected. She stood just within the entrance tunnel where teams would head to their respective locker rooms. Janet didn't look at a sports team, however. A class of 750 students gathered, threw on their robes, then adjusted their mortar boards. Ladies checked their hair and make-up. Administrators nudged students into the proper lines. Colored sashes dropped over the heads of selected people, drawing an embrace between the recipients and the offering faculty.

Janet didn't understand why she stood here. It wasn't the memory she sought when she walked from the soccer pitch. It didn't even match her memory of graduating. Her daughter glowed with pride as she tried to cover the tear streaks that lined her cheeks. She pulled her mortar board from her head and touched a picture of Janet that she'd stashed inside it.

"I miss you, mom. Wish you could be here to see this."

A man from her class walked to her side, gave her a hug. They held each other like close friends. Her daughter released a few sobs, then forced herself to breathe. Janet sensed the man hoped for more from the relationship than her daughter. She and her daughter had discussed relationships before Janet had died. But her daughter had mentioned not feeling ready for any type of long-term commitment. That conversation happened before the start of the most recent semester. Her daughter hadn't said anything more. Even as Janet stood there, she sensed a good, long-term connection. Whether it grew or they remained just good friends, she couldn't tell. A group of five others, mixed genders but an obvious friend cluster, gathered with the two for more hugs and supportive talk. Her daughter had good people taking care of her. Taking a breath, she stepped out of the building.

By passing through the wall, the universe took her to another location. Another scene, but still not one of her memories. It took a minute to orient herself, as nothing appeared right. Instead, she found herself in her living room, though the windows and furniture had black drapes across them. Even in the dim light, the room looked nothing like she'd left it. Her family had removed many of her personal touches. And they'd not cleaned. Dishes gathered on end tables, blankets sat in rumpled piles on the couch.

As she looked around, she realized something else. Her husband occupied space within the room. To suggest he did more than exist, it had no accuracy within that statement. Worse, he looked like he hadn't slept well in days. His physical state didn't speak well of his mental state, either. He lounged on the recliner in his underwear. She couldn't tell if the overall smell emanated from the room. Or from her husband. She'd never seen him in such disarray.

Janet couldn't stay. Leaving her husband, she stepped through the wall to explore more rooms. Her first stop brought her into the kitchen. And stop her, it did. Cabinet doors stood open, papers strewn across the central island. A cell phone sat on the only clear spot of the granite surface, with a notepad beside it. The phone blinked and chirped, with notes about missed calls and texts. Scribbled on the notepad, Janet saw a number and a name: *Mourning Group Therapy*. She reached for the pen to inscribe an additional note, but her fingers passed through the solid object. Maybe her daughters would help snap him out of this funk.

With a slight shake of her head, she walked through the sliding glass doors. She stood on the deck and gazed into the woods behind the house. She leaned on the porch railing and her eyes traced the various leaves. Her hands smacked the railing. Solid, yet she couldn't touch the pen. The physics made no sense, so she let her thoughts wander. How long she stared, she didn't know, but she sensed when another arrived beside her.

"How's the stroll through memory-central?" The voice belonged to Percy, who leaned on the railing beside her.

"I've not looked at a memory since you've left me. All I keep getting are glimpses of the present or coming events." Janet bowed her head. "Everything I see just creates more questions and more confusion. I should stay to help my family."

"That's not one of your choices," Percy said. "If you stay, you'll become a spirit guide for the next wave that passes or you move to the next step. Those still living stop being under our purview." He crossed his wrists and tapped his fingers against the empty air.

Janet pulled her gaze back to the woods. She said nothing, her mind lost in her thoughts of what she faced. Percy remained beside her, silent as she stared. While they stood there, her husband walked from within the house, a mug of tea in his hand. The mug he placed on the railing in front of her, while he leaned on the railing himself, staring at the trees. Did he? No, he couldn't know she stood there. She glanced into the mug and noticed the paleness of the water. He reused his tea bag again. Fifteen minutes passed before he reached for the mug and sipped the tea colored water.

Watching him, Janet became uncomfortable. She pushed herself away from the railing and walked into the yard, settling onto her children's old swing set. Her husband had maintained the piece, for the sake of the grandchildren, but they hadn't received that gift before Janet died. The chains felt cold to her touch, though they didn't squeak as she rocked on them. She imaged it looked like a breeze when her husband looked this way. Something she didn't expect, as she sat there, was Percy and Jerome appearing on the swings to either side of her. As she glanced at Jerome, she tried not to chuckle. He looked more uncomfortable than she felt beside her husband.

"Why does the fact that he lived and I died make me uncomfortable?" Janet wanted to fold her legs under herself, but the swing proved too small.

"It's a way to protect us from active interference with the living," Jerome said. "If we're uncomfortable around the ones we love, we won't want to stay. Or so the theory goes, anyway. Some break the assumptions by sticking around their loved ones, anyway. People think of them as their guardian angels, though all they do is watch." Silence gathered with their group again as they swung with languid motion. Janet's eyes remained on the house, on the desk where her husband stood. Her eyes shifted to the house, as just looking at him made her uncomfortable. She found her eyes drawn back to the mug he held as he stared beyond the swing set. They'd received a set of hot chocolate mugs as a wedding gag gift from his parents. She'd buried them at the back of a cabinet, so he'd gone through a lot of mugs to use that one.

Then another thought occurred to her. The whole staring into the woods had always been her habit, while he'd gone to his office and played video games. To see her husband mirror her habit, she didn't know what she should say or how she should react. His head dipped and his shoulders shook. He'd started crying. Janet wondered how often this scene played out since she'd died. If he still had any tears left. Maybe she shouldn't ask.

As she slipped from the swing, she stretched and looked around, finding the path they'd followed away from the funeral home. No path ever existed among her trees. Janet looked at Percy, both eyebrows raised in unspoken question. He just gestured to the pine needle path.

"It goes where you want it to go, nowhere else," Jerome said. When he looked at her, his eyes held a sad expression she'd not seen when they interacted at the funeral home. Anything away from this house scared Janet. She could admit that to herself now. However, she also knew her family needed to move forward without her. Staying wasn't fair to either of them. Her gaze returned to the path. Maybe as a guide.

"What if I want to go? I mean, work as a guide, but somewhere not in the local area?"

"The path will take you to a place that could use your skills within your energy envelope." Jerome paused. "Or it will guide you toward your next step, if that holds a better place for you."

Janet slid her hands over her outfit, pondered her options. Her eyes locked on the pine needles and on the path. She thought she had this decision made. Every time she tried to move, something made her hold back. Looking over her shoulder, Janet considered Percy and Jerome. They spoke to each other, but each had one eye on Janet. They waited for her to make this decision, too.

After she drew a breath, Janet nodded. She faced the path, closed her eyes, and took the first step. As she entered the path, she knew she'd decided what to do.

Called Home

A light breeze blew the scent of a fresh-fallen rain and the aroma of her perfume in my direction. Her bright-red hair framed her heart-shaped face and expressive green eyes. As her eyes twinkled in the dim starlight, she gazed into my eyes. To appreciate her beauty, I didn't want to look away. We'd dashed down the hill and took that moment to catch our breath.

A minute passed, then she giggled and took my hand. She walked with a light ease along the beach, her bare feet careful to avoid the dry, hot sand. Sunset had just passed, and twilight awaited our teen frolicking. The knee-length, strapless white dress fluttered in the delicate breeze. Her arms and face glistened. Glee filled her face. She glanced back at the resort hall. A dance had started ten minutes before, but we had to leave it. What we were doing, we didn't know. We just knew the dance wasn't for us. Not on such a fine evening. Little did we realize just what this night held for us.

We wandered to the summer resort's border, with the water lapping against the shore. I thought we'd just sit on the sand, but she had other plans. She looked at the dark jetty as the twinkle in her eyes changed. A blush started in her cheeks and flowed throughout her cheeks. She gave me a light kiss on the cheek. With another giggle, she climbed onto the rocks. The breeze shifted as she reached the top of the jetty, blowing everything out to sea. Signs warned people to stay off the rocks, but she ignored them.

"You shouldn't be doing that." My voice had a slight waver as I watched. I wanted to stop her, but I couldn't move without taking my eyes off her lithe form. My feet felt like they were in stiffening, wet cement, glued to the beach. I glanced between the sign and her, getting a knot in my stomach. She threw a glare over her shoulder at me to tell me to quit being an adult. With a giggle, she picked her way along, her dainty feet picking their place carefully among the jagged rocks. She had not gone but a few feet when she slipped. I gasped as her feet slipped out from under her and she landed on her rear with a slight bounce. Turning to see my worried face, she laughed harder. She got to her feet, beckoned me to follow, and started along again.

"Come back. Please. I don't want to see you get hurt."

My voice threatened to catch in my throat. My feet dragged two steps closer to the jetty, though I remained grounded on the beach. She showed nimble grace, didn't need me to help. I shivered as the breeze gusted against my back. Clouds drifted in to obscure the moon. She ignored my comment, continuing along.

When she slipped that second time, I expected the results to repeat themselves. They were, almost, but her hands did not keep their grip. The rocks were too wet and unstable to hold her up. She twisted around to catch herself, but the slime wouldn't allow it. Her head took a harsh, jarring bounce off the rocks, then she rolled into the swirling sea. In moments, she'd disappeared from my sight. I froze, my knees locked. Mortified. I didn't know what to do, so I stared at where she fell.

Go after her! Something told me, but my feet wouldn't move.

Save her! It persisted. No use. I felt frozen, tied in place by seaweed.

Move it, man! It pressed.

It took effort, but I got my feet to work. Clambering to where she fell, I ignored the sign and my safety as much as she did. I scanned the water for any sign of her. Nothing. The cloudy water swirled too much after the recent rains. I stopped just short of where she fell, knelt down, frantically searching for any sign at all. And still Nothing. Not a glimpse of the white dress.

The rock I was on tottered. A sudden gust of wind shoved me forward. I fell, hitting the rock ridge below. Blood clouded my vision. Water gushed about me. After bouncing off the ridge, I fell into the sea. My head felt like someone slammed a sledgehammer against my skull, trying to break through the bone. I couldn't breathe. Sand ground into my teeth. My clothes stuck to my body and what I could feel of my skin was cold and clammy. Everything swirled around me and I lost track of direction. Rocks were everywhere. The longer I tumbled, the more pain raced through my body, my head hitting more rocks below the water's surface.

As I resigned myself to my fate, I felt a tugging from above. Startled, I glanced toward the sensation. She stood there, a hand gripping my shoulder. Her dress flowed with a current that differed from that of the water. She had a glow about her. Her red hair was beautiful as usual, framing her soft radiant face. Her lithe form floated above a rock as she smiled and made several small insistent tugs on my shoulder. My heart leapt, and I moved toward her. The falling ceased. With it, the pain abated. I dropped my gaze behind me and saw my body tumbling with the waves. With a blink of shock, I pulled my gaze back to her. She pointed down the jetty toward the sea, away from my empty shell. There was her shell, her white dress now covered with the filth of the water.

Then began the draw, the pull, from somewhere else. This felt more insistent than when she grabbed my attention, so I knew this wasn't her wanting to move me. It was like rising, but not rising. Like flying, but not flying. I glanced at her just as she smiled and nodded. It was our call home.

Don't miss out!

Visit the website below and you can sign up to receive emails whenever Bert Whirl publishes a new book. There's no charge and no obligation.

https://books2read.com/r/B-A-ZJAX-NCMKC

BOOKS 2 READ

Connecting independent readers to independent writers.

About the Author

Bert Whirl was born in Southern Maryland. He is married to a wonderful wife and works as the servant to three feline overlords. He has not touched AI to create his works. He's enjoyed enough science fiction to hope for Data but fears we'll get Skynet, Sentinels, and VIKI.